VITO'S EUROPEAN TRAVELS
Segovia and Ronda, Spain

I0627423

BY

VITO AMORELLI

Copyright © 2024

ISBN

978-1-964818-26-9

978-1-964818-27-6

978-1-964818-28-3

All Rights Reserved. Any unauthorized reprint or use of this material is strictly prohibited. No part of this book may be reproduced or transmitted in any form or by any means, electronic or mechanical, including photocopying, recording, or by any information storage and retrieval system without express written permission from the author.

All reasonable attempts have been made to verify the accuracy of the information provided in this publication. Nevertheless, the author assumes no responsibility for any errors and/or omissions.

DEDICATION

This book is dedicated to Leslie Seifried because without her encouragement getting me on a plane while kicking and screaming, I would never have seen or photographed as much of Europe as I have. Every time I crossed the threshold from the gangway to the plane, all I kept thinking is "Why do I keep doing this to myself". Her patience and understanding of my fear of flying made my experiences and these photos possible. As Ibn Balluta, a 14th Century Moroccan Traveler said, "Travel makes us speechless, then it turns you into a storyteller". There are many stories of greatness and sadness in the places and architectures, sights and sounds of places other than our own homes. It is one thing to read about them in dry history books, it is quite another to actually experience them. I would have experienced none of them if not for Leslie. If my photographs can inspire one person to go to one place, the time and effort of these books and videos will be worth it.

Ronda
Created by the forces of nature

Ronda is a mountaintop city in Spain sitting on top of a deep gorge.

The town was first settled by the early Celts, in the 6th century,

later by Phoenician and Roman settlers who set it up as a fortified post in the Second Punic War.

MVSEO LARA

HEAVEN
IRISH TAVERN

The town is divided by the gorge separating the city's 15th-century new town from its old town, dating to Moorish conquest.

TIENDA
Shop

It was reconquered by the Catholic forces of Ferdinand and Isabella, in 1485.

Most of the city's old edifices were renewed or adapted to Christian rule, but you can still see Moorish influences throughout the town.

The Plaza de Toros (bullring) was built entirely of stone in the 18th century. It was actually completed before the one in Sevilla, which is considered the oldest. However, part of the stands collapsed on its opening and therefore wasn't considered operational.

From the park there
are amazing views of
the valley below. Hard
for an enemy to sneak
up on you.

The gorge is called "El Tajo" and was created by constant erosion of the river Guadalevín.

You can get to some of the different levels but this view is amazing.

The shear size of
the gorge also has
a tendency to make
you feel very small.

During the Islamic period,
Ronda was considered
the "Rose of the
Kingdom of Granada".

In 1349, the black death killed many of Ronda's citizens. There was only one supply of water, so the disease easily swept through the small city.

In 1485 the Christian army surrounded the city and cut off its water supply so the city surrendered after the short siege.

Vincent Espinel was born in 1550 in Ronda. He was responsible for adding the fifth string to the guitar, called vihuela. This led to the creation of the Spanish guitar.

In the early 19th century, the Napoleonic invasion reduced the citizenry from 15,600 to 5,000 in just three years.

In Hemingway's "For Whom the Bell Tolls", during the Spanish Civil War the Republicans murder the Nationalists by throwing them from cliffs in an Andalusian village, and he supposedly based the executions on actual killings on the cliffs of Ronda.

In 1987 the ashes of Orson Wells were brought to Ronda and buried in an old well.

Segovia
A trip back in time

AMBULANCIA
ASISTENCIAL
112
1782 HSP

Traveling to Segovia is like a step back in time.Its amazing that a community so tucked away in the Spanish countryside could have had such an effect and been so important to an empire thousands of miles away.

The name Segovia
is of Celtic origins.

ES OBLIGATORIO SEGUIR TODAS
LAS NORMAS DE SEGURIDAD
PROHIBIDO EL PASO A TODA
PERSONA AJENA A LA OBRA

The Roman aqueduct was built around 50BC with around 24,000 mostly original mortarless granite stones from the Guadarrama Mountains and comprises over 167 arches.

❧"EL ALCÁZAR, QVE PERTENECIÓ
SIEMPRE AL CVERPO DE ARTILLERÍA,
DESEO VUELVA OTRA VEZ A SU PODER"

S. M. ALFONSO XIII, 6 D MAYO D MCMVIII ❧

Only Keystones and gravity keep this structure standing.

Each stone was specifically quarried for its position in the structure.

Parts of the aqueduct were used until 1973

It wasn't until the early 1990s that traffic was stopped from driving so close to the structure due to vibrations weakening the structure.

It is believed that the city was abandoned after the Islamic invasion of Spain. After the conquest of Toledo, Segovia was resettled with Christians from the north of the Iberian Peninsula and beyond the Pyrenees.

Segovia's position on trading routes made it an important centre of trade in wool and textiles.

EL 13 DE DICIEMBRE
DE 1474
EN EL ATRIO DE LA IGLESIA DE S MIGUEL
LA CIUDAD DE SEGOVIA
PROCLAMO REINA DE CASTILLA
A ISABEL LA CATOLICA
R. 1984

Castle Alcázar de Segovia has been around since the 12th Century.

It has been a prison, a royal artillery college, a military academy, and now a museum

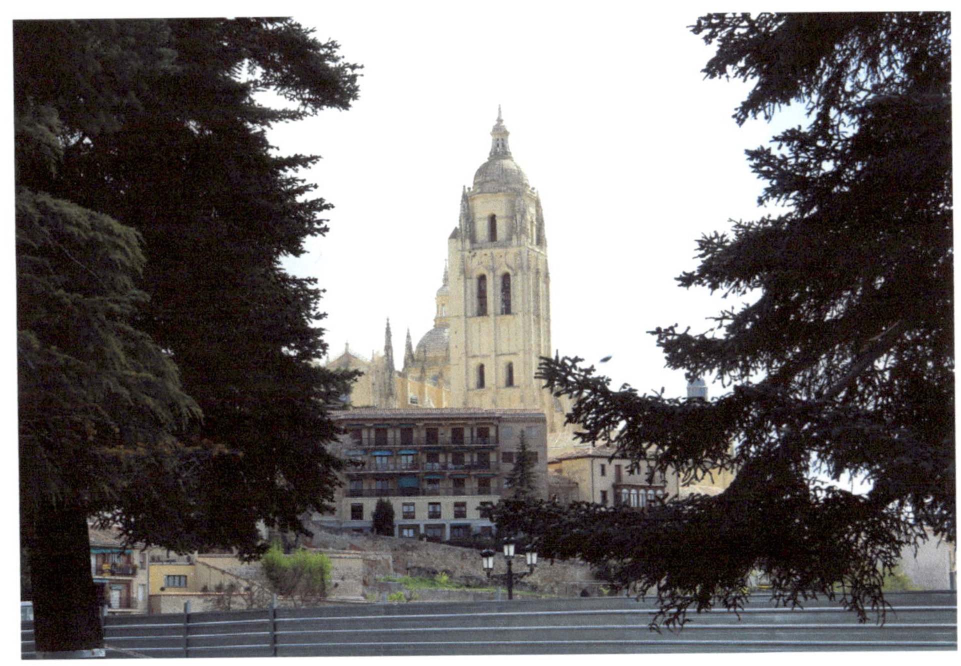

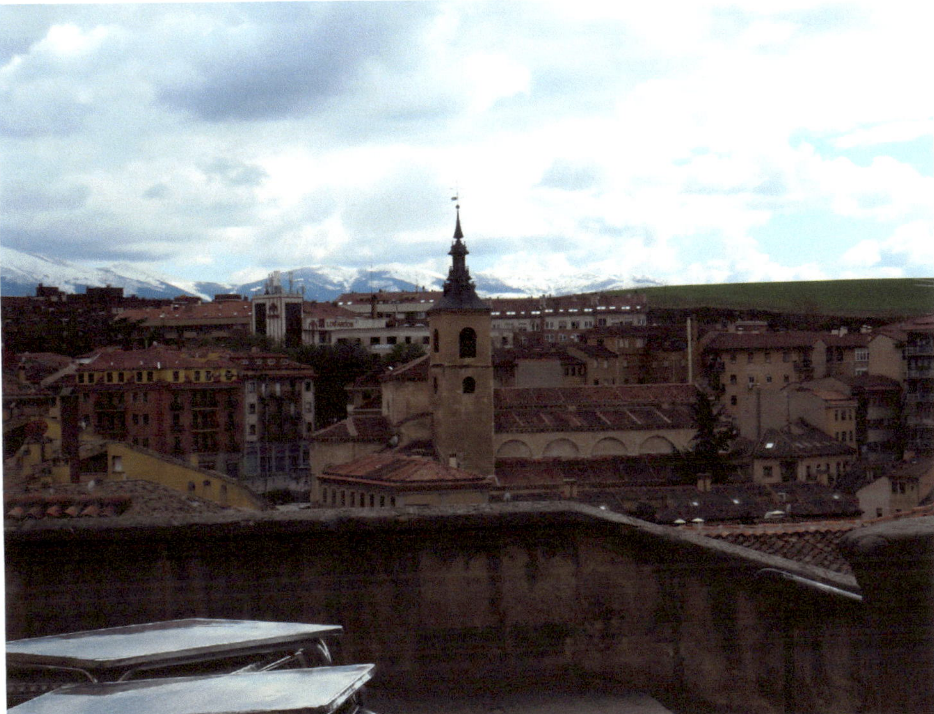

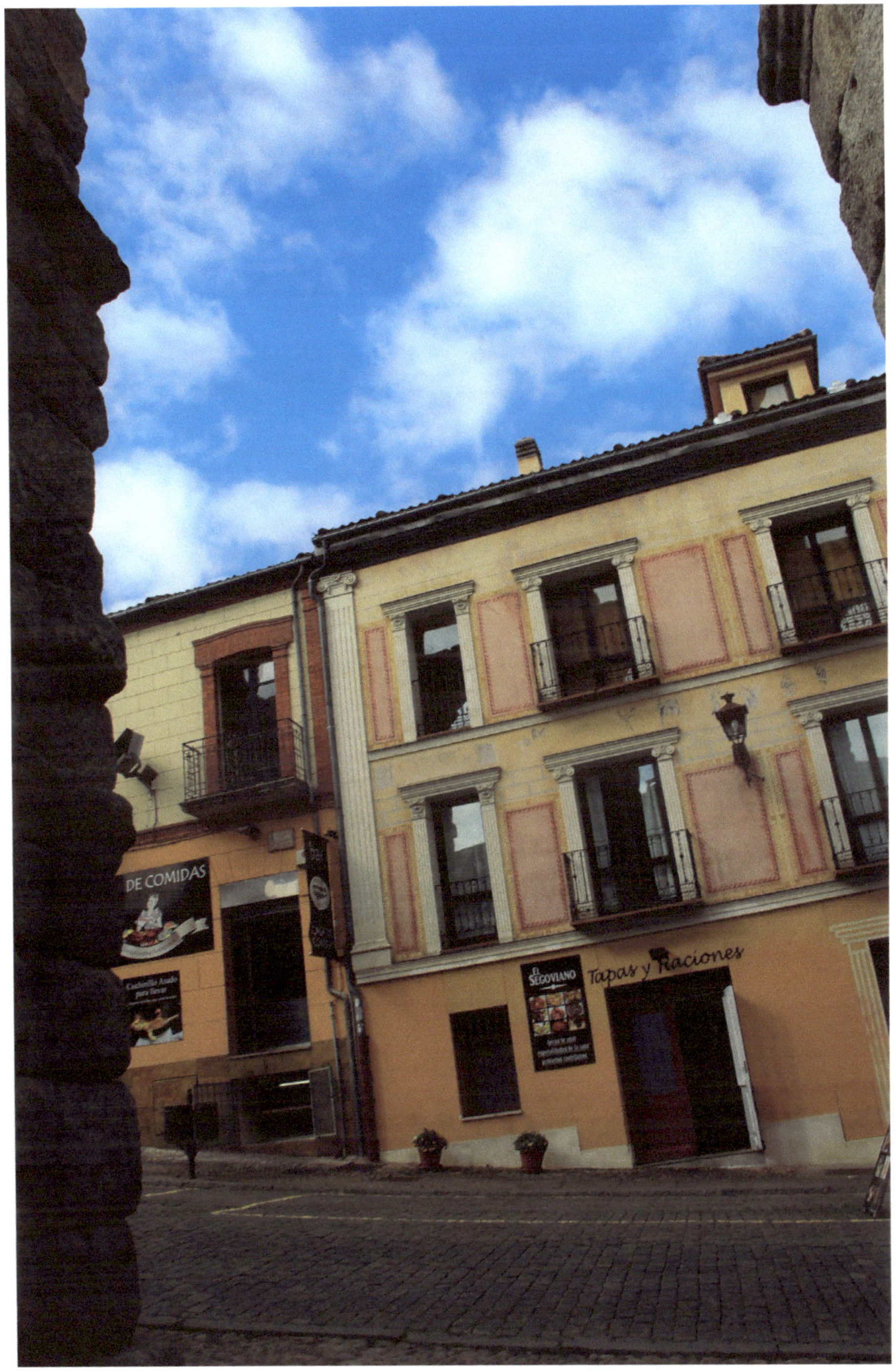
DE COMIDAS
Cochinillo Asado para llevar
EL SEGOVIANO
Tapas y Raciones

ROMA
A
SEGOVIA
EN EL
BIMILEÑARIO
DE SU
AGUEDUCTO
MCMLXXIV

SEGOVIA
A
JUAN BRAVO
1921

CAPILLA
DE Sⁿ JUAN
DE DIOS

It was here the groundwork for the formation of the modern Spanish nation, took place.

Isabel the Catholic, left the Alcazar to proclaim herself queen of Castile.

It was also the site of the last meeting between Christopher Columbus and King Ferdinand before Columbus's death.

The castle has great views from
its walls and courtyards.
The Church of San Martin in
Segovia is a 12th-century church
built in a Moorish style.
Segovia Cathedral was built at
the highest point of the town
starting in 1525 and is the last
Gothic cathedral built in Spain.

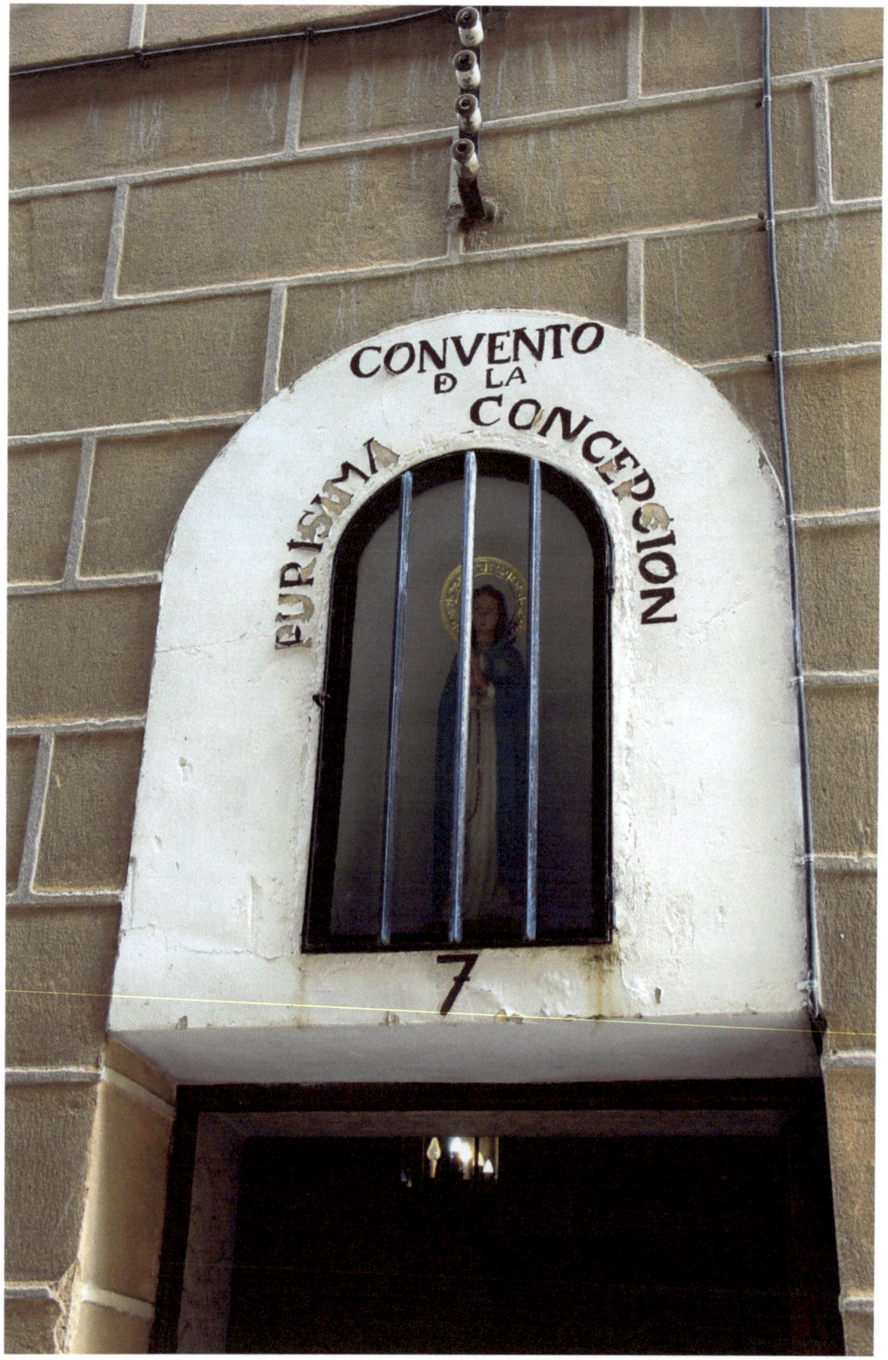

CONVENTO
Ð LA
PURISMA CONCEPCION
7

About the author:

Vito is a photographer, singer, songwriter, and musician. Raised in a small town in central Massachusetts and playing a variety of musical instruments, he was influenced like many of his generation by the British Invasion of the mid-60s. Picking up a guitar, joined a band and started writing his own music until entering the Army. Vito's tours in Vietnam in 1967 and 1968, taught him that there was an entire world separate from the one he grew up in and it sparked an interest to see the places he had read about since he was seven. Although his interest in photography was more of a hobby, it really didn't begin to develop until he started traveling after retiring. He has gathered numerous collections of unique & inspiring photos from domestic and international travels. His European collection includes the classics as well as the unexpected from time spent in Italy, France, Switzerland, Germany, Spain, Austria, Croatia, Monaco, Portugal, Ireland, Scotland, and England.

With an artistic eye, Vito's work has wide appeal and provides interest in both residential and commercial settings. Vito's photographs have been on display in local studios, car dealerships, city halls, and used for staging in the Boston real estate market. He has held art shows and displayed his photos at the French Cultural Center in Boston. As a member of Broadsword the Band, has five CD's on IHeart Radio, Amazon, Apple Music, and iTunes, as well as music and travel videos on YouTube.

This coffee table book is two of the many places visited and photographed. Segovia and Ronda, Spain.

www.ingramcontent.com/pod-product-compliance
Lightning Source LLC
Chambersburg PA
CBHW041344300726
48978CB00004B/139